SEN SUPERPOWERS

The Map Challenge
a book about dyslexia

Written by
Dr. Tracy Packiam Alloway

Illustrated by
Ana Sanfelippo

It was the first day of scout camp.
Sammy and his friends were so excited
they raced around the campsite.

2

"This is going to be the best scout camp ever!" Sammy cheered.

"Red group, your mission is a flag hunt," said scout leader Jess. "Follow the map to find your team flag and bring it back to camp before dark."

"Sammy, you can be the navigator,"
said scout leader Matt, handing him a map.

Sammy felt a lump in his throat. He slowly unfolded the
big map but the words just danced around the paper.

Sammy felt sick at the thought of trying to navigate.
"Could I have a different job?" he whispered.
But no one heard—they were too busy getting ready.

Poor Sammy, the words on the map were all jumbled up! Nadia snickered. "Sammy's holding the map upside down," she said.

"I think we have to go **up** the path," Sammy stammered. Daisy peered over his shoulder at the map. "Wrong," she said. "We have to go **down** the path."

The scouts headed off down the path toward their team flag. Dawdling at the back, Sammy spotted an old well.

Sammy felt sure a troll was hiding at the bottom of the well so he hurried on.

7

"Let's go north," said Sammy.

"I think we are lost," said Tim, as he sat down in something squishy.

Determined to navigate, Sammy led everyone through a gate and into a field. SNORT! A bull suddenly thundered toward them...

"I don't think this is north," yelled Daisy. "Run!"

Daisy took over as navigator and led them back to the path. Sammy noticed a bright red bird chirping in its nest. He tried to whistle the tune.

"If we turn **left** here, the path should lead us toward the flag," said Daisy.

But Sammy didn't hear her. He was too busy looking at the mossy rocks. Next to the rocks were some bright red, spotted toadstools.

Sammy blinked quickly. Click, click, just like a camera. The pictures were now saved in his memory.

The path led to a bridge.

"Can anyone see the flag?
It should be right here," said Dylan.

"I can't see it," whined Tim.
"It must be here somewhere!" Daisy said.

But Sammy wasn't listening. He was following a trail of ants he had spotted on the bridge. When he looked up he saw the flag peeking out from behind a bush. Yay! He grabbed the flag.

"Woo hoo!" Tim cheered, "Sammy found the flag!"

13

Suddenly a gust of wind whipped the map out of Dylan's hand . . . and into the river!

14

"Now how will we find our way?"
wailed Dylan. "We're lost!"

Sammy's heart was doing somersaults.

He forgot about up and down.
He forgot about left and right,
or north and south. He just
thought about the places he
had saved in his memory.

15

"Follow me," Sammy said. "I'll show you the way."

"Past the mossy rocks and red spotted toadstools."

"Around the tree with the chirping bird."

"Past the bull in the field.
Shhh, we don't want to wake him!"

"Past the old well."

As they passed a bush, there was a loud rustling sound. "What's that?" squealed Dylan, grabbing Sammy's arm.

A squirrel jumped out in front of them. "Don't be scared," said Sammy. "We're nearly back!"

Then, out of the corner of
his eye, Sammy saw something
red among the bushes.
"Over here!" he said.
"It's the campsite sign!"

19

"Sammy, you did it!" yelled Daisy.
"We made it!" Nadia shouted. "We're safe!"

"How did you navigate without a map?"
asked Tim, as the scouts all looked at Sammy.
Sammy smiled. "I saved all the places in my memory!"

"Hurray!" cheered the scouts.
"Who needs a map when we have Sammy!"

NOTES FOR PARENTS AND TEACHERS

Dyslexia is a common learning difficulty that can cause problems with certain abilities used for learning such as:

READING

Dyslexic children often describe how words "jump around" on the page and get mixed up with different letters (such as "b" and "d," or "p" and "q"). As a result of the extra effort they have to spend when reading, they often forget what they read.

NAVIGATION

Children with dyslexia can find navigation and map reading difficult because they often mix up left/right, up/down, and north/south/east/west. This can happen even in familiar places, environments, and routes.

MEMORY

Dyslexic children often have poor verbal working memory. This means they have difficulty remembering sequences of information presented out loud, such as instructions, new vocabulary, and names.

For more information, visit The International Dyslexia Association website: www.dyslexiaida.org

Try to consider the suitability of tasks that you give to a dyslexic child. They might find reading and navigation tricky, but, just like Sammy, children with dyslexia have strong visual memory.

This skill means that they are great at remembering things that they see, such as landmarks and images.

DISCUSSION POINTS ABOUT THE STORY

Explain to the children what dyslexia is and that it can have an impact on reading, writing, and spelling skills. Also talk about the many positive aspects of having dyslexia, such as being creative, curious, and imaginative. Below are some discussion points about the story that will help children with their comprehension skills as well as developing their awareness of dyslexia:

(p4) How do you think Sammy felt when he was asked to be the navigator?

(pp10-13) Sammy noticed lots of things that his friends didn't. How did he lead his group back to the camp without a map?

(p6) Sammy struggled to read the map. Why do you think he found it hard? Have you ever struggled with a task?

(pp20-21) Sammy led the group back to the campsite and saved the day. How do you think he felt at the end of the story? How do you think Sammy's friends felt?

TIPS FOR BOOSTING MEMORY SKILLS

Here are some handy tips and ideas to help children be superheroes like Sammy!

BE A BIRD
To help find a way back to an original starting point, encourage children to imagine the journey from a bird's-eye view.

WALK THE WALK
To support navigation skills, tell children to imagine themselves walking through the route. When they actually make the journey, they will have already done it once in their heads so it should seem more familiar.

MOVE IT!
Studies show that when we move while we learn, we are more likely to remember the information.

TURN IT UP!
Listening to music while learning can help the brain remember what is being learned.

PUZZLE ME THIS
Jigsaw puzzles are a great way to develop the ability to see patterns. They can also help to boost spatial ability—the power to understand and remember the spatial relations between objects.

Quarto is the authority on a wide range of topics.
Quarto educates, entertains and enriches the lives of our readers—enthusiasts and lovers of hands-on living.
www.quartoknows.com

Author: Dr. Tracy Packiam Alloway
Illustrator: Ana Sanfelippo
Editors: Rachel Moss and Emily Pither
Designers: Clare Barber and Victoria Kimonidou
Consultant: Lorraine Petersen OBE

© 2019 Quarto Publishing plc

First published in 2019 by QEB Publishing, an imprint of The Quarto Group.
6 Orchard Road, Suite 100
Lake Forest, CA 92630
T: +1 949 380 7510
F: +1 949 380 7575
www.QuartoKnows.com

A CIP record for this book is available from the Library of Congress.

ISBN 978-1-78603-577-6

Manufactured in Shenzhen, China PP052019
9 8 7 6 5 4 3 2 1

MIX
Paper from responsible sources
FSC® C001701

To my funny superhero Magnus, who finds creative solutions to problems.